A Game of Two Halves

OTHER OXFORD FICTION

How to Survive Summer Camp
Jacqueline Wilson

Simone's Letters
Helena Pielichaty

Cool Clive, the coolest kid alive
Michaela Morgan

The Worst Team in the World
Alan MacDonald

Temmi and the Flying Bears
Stephen Elboz

The Bongleweed
Helen Cresswell

The Piemakers
Helen Cresswell

Del sat silent. Soon it was his stop.
'See you at seven, Del!' yelled Senna
as Del got up.

'Yeah,' shouted Spanner. 'Don't go
missing. WE WANT OUR MEDALS!'

Del watched the flickering bus lights slip away into the gloom. Spanner's words echoed in his head.

We want our medals. Is that me, he thought – MR MEDALS?

There were other things he liked to do: playing on his keyboard and his computer and just messing about. Life wasn't only football.

But football had taken him over.

There was the school team in midweek,
City Juniors on Saturdays and
Steelhouse Blues on Sundays.

And then there was Dad.

Rod Taylor was ex-England, ex-
United, but he was still good – he now
played for City.

And there was Harry Green, running City Juniors on Saturdays and Steelhouse on Sundays.

How many games had Del played since he was seven? How many goals had he scored? Dad knew.

He had played two hundred and seven games and scored nine hundred and ninety-seven goals. Dad wrote it all down in a book.

'That lad's a genius! Better than his dad,' Harry Green had said, again and again.

Del was sick of hearing it. He wasn't sick of football. He wasn't sick of the lovely swish as the ball hit the net. Just sick of the pressure and shouting and questions. Tired of Harry Green screeching and roaring even though Steelhouse never lost.

CHAPTER 2

'Come on, Del!'

An hour after Del arrived home, his dad was already looking at his watch.

'All set?' said his dad.

'Okay.'

'What's the matter? Aren't you feeling well?'

'I'm okay, Dad.'

'Is it nerves?'

I just want to be left alone, thought Del. But he said, 'I'm okay.'

'Well, I hope so. It's a big night tonight.'

'I know.'

'A lot of important people will be watching you.'

'I know.'

'Aren't you interested?'

Dad's voice had that edge again. Things had not gone so well recently for City. The senior team had been losing and now Del could tell his dad wasn't pleased with him. The footballer's green eyes were shining with irritation.

'Yes, Dad, but...' He started to explain what he was feeling, but his dad wasn't listening.

'I don't understand you. When I was your age...' Del closed his eyes. Dad's voice played the same record again and again.

Steelhouse hadn't lost for three years.
He had already scored hundreds of
goals. What more did Dad want?
'Yes, Dad.'

'... I'd have given anything to be as
good as you...'
'Yes, Dad.'
'It took me years, years...'
'Yes, Dad.'

'Loads of kids would give their right arm to be as good as you...'

'Sorry, Dad.' Del felt guilty, just the way he did when his gran told him about all those starving children in Africa when he didn't finish his lunch.

The phone rang to save him.

'Del, it's for you – Spanner,' Mum called.

Good old Spanner! Getting him off the hook!

'Are you ready?' shouted Spanner. 'I am. I'm so excited… And Mum's washed the shirts TWICE!'

'Wonderful,' said Del. 'We'll be the cleanest team in the league.'

'Ha! That's a good one!' Spanner laughed. 'See you at seven.'

Del put the phone down.

His dad cut in quickly. 'And another thing…'

BEEP – BEEP!

Del picked the phone up again.

'Del? Harry here. You still all right for tonight?'

'Yes, Harry,' sighed Del. 'I'm all right.'

He put the phone down.

'As I was saying…' Dad tried again.

BEEP – BEEP!

This time it was Senna, the goalie.

Del put the phone down again. It's only football! he thought. They've all gone mad.

Soon it was time to go. He slipped upstairs for his bag. The medals hanging on the wall reminded him of what Spanner had said on the bus. *We want our medals*. He stood staring at them.

But not for long. His Dad's voice came up the stairs. 'Come on, Del! I'm waiting.'

It wasn't far to the stadium, twenty minutes in his dad's car. Dad drove without speaking. Del was glad. His mind was a jumble of mixed-up thoughts.

Who am I doing this for? Me? The lads? Dad? This is mad! I should be loving it. Everybody thinks I do. And I do – sometimes.

'Here now.' His dad's sharp voice popped the bubble of his thoughts.

Up ahead of them were the great concrete hills of the stands with the silent, steel giraffes of the floodlights watching over them. The giant indoor sports complex was round the back.

As soon as they saw Del, everyone
wanted to talk to him.

Harry Green was boasting again.
'We'll hammer them. Just give it to Del
and we'll walk it!' The coach had run
Steelhouse for twenty years and he had
never had a great team before. Then Del
Taylor changed all that.

Spanner ran up. 'I'm dreaming!' he said, grinning from ear to ear. 'I'm in a CUP FINAL at City's ground!'

Del and Spanner had been friends ever since they were little. It was hard not to like Spanner. He was so keen.

Secretly, Del wondered why Spanner liked playing football so much. He was hopeless. He had never even scored in a proper match!

The two boys were very different. Del had always been quiet. He was a bit of a loner. Spanner was always joking. He was so good tempered that he put everyone in a good mood. But tonight, Del found it hard to grin, even at his friend.

Del just sat staring. He knew what he could do. Trouble was, he didn't want to do it any more. He felt more alone than he had ever done in his life.

CHAPTER 3

'Leave me alone'

The others were used to Del sitting by himself. Del always concentrated, always sat quietly before a match. The quiet before the storm of goals. They'd never seen anyone like Del.

But when Del sat alone this time it was different. He had made up his mind. This was going to be his last game. But how would he tell everyone? How would he tell Dad? That was the problem.

Everyone else was excited. Spanner went to the toilet five times. The other players grinned. They could see their medals in front of them already.

Soon it was time for Steelhouse to run on to the pitch, collars up, with Del leading the way.

Vernon Park crept on, goggling at the great glass-domed roof and massive emerald pitch.

Then they eyed Del. He was juggling the ball, flicking it right over his head, then back-heeling it over to halt, once again, on his foot. They remembered the four goals from last time.

Del looked up and saw his dad wave from the gallery bar. It was packed out with scouts looking for new talent. His dad must have told them to come.

And so the Stockdale Under-12s Cup Final began. You could tell the game had started, not only because the ref had blown, but because Harry Green had started his dance on the touchline.

'Hit it! Hold it! Push it! LEAVE IT! For heaven's sake!'

He ranted like a mad parrot. His favourite screech was 'Give it to Del!'

But Del made sure that he was running the same way as his marker all the time. He didn't touch the ball for ages.

Then, disaster! Steelhouse were too confident and they were careless. As they attacked, they left only one defender in place, Porky.

Suddenly, Vernon Park played the ball quickly downfield. Porky tripped and a nippy little striker ran on all alone to score easily.

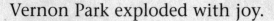

Vernon Park exploded with joy.

Steelhouse had red faces all round, especially Senna the goalie. He had only let five in all season.

A couple of Steelhouse players glared at Del as if it was his fault they were losing.

'Come on, Del. Do something!' snapped Cropper their big defender. 'We're normally three-up by now!'

'COME ON!' Now Harry Green was leaping up and down. 'For heaven's sake, Del! Get on with it!'

Then the chance came. Del captured a careless pass from the Vernon sweeper. Their keeper was out on the edge of the box. Their goal gaped like the Channel Tunnel.

'Hit it!' yelled Cropper.

'Hit it!' screamed Cyrus.

'Have a go, Del!' squeaked Spanner.

'For goodness sake, hit it!!' ranted Harry Green almost chewing the turf.

But Del didn't hit it, he put his foot on the ball and stood still.

'What's he doing?' Harry Green's glasses had misted over. 'The lad's gone potty!!'

The Vernon keeper took advantage of the miracle to run like mad towards his goal.

The big Vernon sweeper who had made the mistake ran at Del. But – *flick* – with one neat kick Del lifted the ball over the boy's head and ran past him.

Then the keeper charged out. *Flick* – and the ball flew over his head.

Del ran round the back of him, caught the ball on his right foot and rolled it gently into the open goal.

The whole place burst out clapping and cheering. Even some of the Vernon Park lads joined in. It was football magic – the way they play in Brazil. But this was only Stockdale and Del Taylor.

'A genius!' shouted Harry Green. 'What did I tell you? A genius.'

Del walked back to the centre spot, cool as ice.

Now leave me alone, he thought.

He looked up seriously at his dad and raised a hand slightly. Their eyes met. His dad looked puzzled.

CHAPTER 4

Penalty!

Half-time was full of excitement.
Vernon Park looked worried. Steelhouse
were buzzing, eyes shining. It was still
1–1, but they were on their way. They
had Del!

Del sat quietly as usual. His mind was
made up.

'Take them apart, Del!' said big
Cropper. 'We can put six past them this
time.'

Spanner just patted him on the arm
with stars in his eyes.

The second half started with Del playing back in defence.

'Get up there, Del!' Harry was screaming and waving him forward to the attack.

Del looked up and saw his dad's face high up above the scoreboard. He thought Dad too might go mad, waving him upfield. But no, his dad was standing with his hand on his chin, looking thoughtful.

Del drifted back and back and back. This meant that Del was there to stop Vernon Park scoring. But Steelhouse didn't score either.

There was less than ten minutes left of the game. Something had to happen. Then a Vernon defender kicked a high ball downfield. The ball skidded off a Steelhouse knee.

Corner!

'Back, lads!' yelled Harry. 'Five minutes left! Get ready for the corner.'

Del jogged into position and glanced up again. No Dad!

The kick was taken just as Del's dad walked into the arena. The ball fizzed hard and low across the goal mouth.

It clipped someone's heel and flicked up on to Del's hand.

'PENALTY!!!!!!!'

The ref was pointing at the penalty
spot and the place was in uproar.

'You DUCK EGG, DEL!'

Cropper was face to face with him.
He looked ready to punch him.

'It hit me – right? I'm not Superman!'
said Del as he walked away with his
back to everyone.

'Give me strength!!' roared Harry.
'He's blown it for us, now. We're going
to lose!'

In went the penalty. 2–1 to Vernon
Park.

Five more minutes, thought Del, as
he trailed back to the centre. Then it's
over. No more football for me.

Then he heard his dad's voice.

'DEL!'

He glanced across. He saw the sad
look in his dad's eye and walked across
to be shouted at, as usual.

Up at the bar window, City players
were grinning and pulling faces. Del
thought he heard someone laugh,
'Wonder-boy! Wonder-boy!'

Why couldn't they just let him be?
Why couldn't they leave him to enjoy
his football instead of expecting him to
be some kind of goal machine?

On the Vernon Park bench everyone
was laughing too. His dad looked
terrible.

'Dad?'

'Don't worry, son. I saw what
happened...' Then he patted Del on the
shoulder. 'Never mind... it wasn't your
fault. Show them what you can do!' He
gave his City team mates a nasty look as
he jerked a thumb towards them.

As Del walked back to the middle,
the eyes of all his mates
arrowed into him.
He could almost feel
their angry thoughts.

This was why he wasn't going to play
again. Ever.

Then, as he came up to the centre
circle, Spanner ran over to him. Poor
Spanner! There'd be no winner's medal
for him today after all. But he wasn't
angry with Del.

'It wasn't your fault, Del!' he said
loyally. 'You'll show them, won't you?
Look, their keeper's off his line again!'
    Del took a crafty look. Spanner was
right.

The Vernon keeper had run out cheering when they scored the penalty. He was still way out, joking with a defender – the idiot!

Now, with three minutes remaining, there was no time for circus tricks like before.

The jeers of the City team swirled round in Del's head. Suddenly, he was angry. Yes, he'd show them.

'Touch it to me, Span!' he said.

Spanner kicked off. Del took the ball and he was away. Five steps inside the Vernon half, he smashed the ball over the keeper's head...

...and into the back of the net. 2–2.

The teams kicked off again. And, before the Vernon team had finished arguing, Spanner sent Del his first straight pass of the evening. With the ball under perfect control, Del swerved left, and then right, past four defenders.

Then he fooled the goal keeper into diving the wrong way and ran neatly past him.

Del could easily have put the ball into the open net. But he didn't, he stopped.

The defenders all ran at him, desperately. Spanner was charging up alone on the other side like a mad horse. Del carefully sidefooted the ball right across the face of the goal.

Even Spanner could not miss from less than a metre out.

The stadium exploded with yells of disbelief. Spanner was mobbed by the excited Steelhouse team as he bounded round the pitch waving his arms and shouting.

YEHHAHHHHH!!!!

The last minute crawled round as Del took the ball and kept it under his control until the whistle went. 3–2 to Steelhouse!

The whole Steelhouse team went mad, cheering and shouting. That is – all except Del. He stood in the centre circle, his heart thundering with excitement.

This is special, he thought. I'll always remember today! And Spanner, who hadn't turned on him after that penalty. Even though he wanted his medal more than anything. Spanner was a real friend.

But he also remembered the jeerers in the City team who were now cheering their heads off. For a whole minute he stared and stared at them, stony-faced.

Then he joined the Steelhouse lads on their lap of honour. Everyone wanted to praise him. Could he turn his back on this? But this was only when you won, wasn't it?

Cropper came up, head bowed. 'Sorry about yelling at you, Del. I was out of order,' he said. 'You were fantastic!'

CHAPTER 5

The winner

Soon everyone had their medals and Del was on his way home. His dad was glowing with pride.

'Brilliant, just brilliant,' he said. 'You gave it to Spanner on purpose, didn't you? You set it up because he's your friend! He's the worst player on the team, isn't he?'

Del just laughed.

'He scored though, didn't he?'

Good old Spanner!

'Okay?' said his mum when they arrived back.

'Fantastic!' said his dad. 'He's better than I ever was!'

'What do you want for supper, Del?' asked his mum. 'Something special for a winner?'

'No, Mum, I'm tired. I'll just have a cup of tea.'

And off he went to his room to flop on his bed. On went his Walkman. The booming music might stop the thoughts whizzing about in his head. But it was no good. He felt so restless that he couldn't stand up or sit down and feel comfortable.

He thought he heard a creak on the stairs, but decided it was nothing. Then he stood staring at his wall of souvenirs and photographs. Time to go to bed maybe?

He tried to take his tracksuit top off
without removing the medal from
round his neck. The ribbon snapped
and the gold prize spun on to the floor.

But he didn't pick it up. He peeled off
his shirt, walked towards the window,
walked back then stopped in front of
the fallen medal.

At that moment, his dad walked in
with a cup of tea, picked up the medal
and handed it and the tea to Del with a
sad smile.

'Plenty more to come, eh?'

Del said nothing. I'm never going to
be able to tell him, he thought. His dad
sat next to him on the bed.

'Funny thing, people,' started his dad.
'Like those lads back at the club.
Thought I knew them...'

What's he talking about? thought
Del. What's he getting at?

'What are you trying to tell me, Dad?'

'… Then I realized, tonight. How much they rate people just because they're winners.' His dad hesitated.

'Well, football's been my whole life and football up there is about winning, just winning. But I saw your face after that penalty… heard those jeering idiots in the bar… Then I saw your medal on the floor just now and I realized that I'm no better than them.'

'No, Dad! There are always people like that at matches, I'm used to it…' Del started.

'Thanks, son, but you're wrong to make excuses for me. I'm not "people", I'm your DAD, Del! I want you to do... what you like doing... If you choose to do something else... well... it's all right by me, okay?'

He patted Del on the shoulder and he stood up without looking the boy in the eye. It had been hard to say it, Del knew.

The big, strong footballer started towards the door.

Del's voice stopped him.

'Thanks, Dad!'

His dad turned and without another word went downstairs.

For a second, Del felt a ton lighter.

I don't have to play any more! he thought. I'm free!

But then he felt empty. He remembered the lovely feeling as the ball flies off your foot into the net. And then there was everyone else on the team.

He walked across his room to the shield on the wall and draped the medal over it with all the others. When he was over there the Steelhouse team photo caught his eye.

He imagined the glowing faces of the lads tonight. Cropper, Porky, Senna, Cyrus and especially Spanner, would be at home now, waving their medals about, telling their mums and dads all about it.

Then ringing their uncles and aunties and friends to repeat it all over again.

But the one that stood out was Spanner, tall and blond and lanky, left-footed and played down the right! Useless, but mad keen... only on the team because his mum ran a launderette. And now he was a hero! Because of Del.

After the presentation, Spanner had come up to Del with tears in his eyes and given him a big hug.

'Del,' he said, 'this is the best day of my whole life…' and then his voice had faded away.

Del stared hard at the picture – at Spanner's bony chest puffed out in pride and the horrible wire glasses that he'd forgotten to take off for the team photo.

Okay, Spanner, you win! he thought.

He smiled, scratched his head, put his boots and trainers under his bed, walked to the door and called downstairs.

'Hey, Dad, who are we playing on Saturday?'

The
Booming Boots
of Joey Jones

DAVID CLAYTON

Illustrated by Stephen Player

OXFORD
UNIVERSITY PRESS

CHAPTER 1

Joe feels lucky

Joey Jones was a laugh, everyone knew that. He didn't really mean to be funny. He was just a one-man disaster zone. No matter how many times he tried to succeed, something always seemed to go wrong.

Joe thought about it a lot. Was he clumsy or just unlucky? Sometimes he wondered. Maybe there was always some banana skin out there ready to trip him. Joe didn't know.

It was like the time he messed things up for Tank at the inter-schools swimming gala. Tank was a good swimmer and was winning the free-style final. But Tank just had to be in the outside lane. And Joe just had to go mad and lean over too far just as he trod on his slippery goggles.

Tank wasn't expecting to be dive-bombed. Their meeting ten metres from the finish was the highlight of the evening. The kids laughed. The parents laughed. Even the teachers laughed. Tank did not laugh. Joe never heard the last of his blunder. Tank never forgot that Joe had made him look a fool.

However, just before Christmas, Joe got his chance. He had, at long last, got on to the school football team, and football was king at Newton Hall.

It happened like this. His school was due to play Flowery Field in the cup semi-finals. But there was a problem. Newton was the smallest school in the area. There was always a bit of a gap to fill if anyone was off, as they had so few players to choose from. Now, to make things worse, flu had struck and half the kids were missing.

A week before the game, on practice day, Mr Murphy told Joe the good news.

He bounced into the changing room grinning.

'I'm lucky! So very, very lucky!' Joe said to himself.

The teacher looked carefully at Joe – at his wide grin and big boots.

'We really need you, Joe,' he said. 'But no muck-ups, eh?'

'I won't let you down, sir!' said the boy.

Tank, the team captain, scowled.
'What do we want him for?' he
muttered. 'He's rubbish!'
But Joe's luck had changed. Or had it?

As they went out into the afternoon gloom, he had a good look at the team. It was all odds and ends like a box of liquorice allsorts.

There was speedy little Eddy Morgan, big fat Arthur who almost filled his goal, and red-faced Tank with legs like sausages. Joe noticed, too, that even his skinny friend, Skenner Skelly, was playing for the first time.

The girls doing gymnastics in the hall sniggered at the ragged army as it set out into the sleet. They were in the warm.

However, nothing bothered Joe. He would have played at midnight at the North Pole for a chance like this. So out he ran, on to the school pitch as if it were Wembley. He imagined the crowd chanting, 'Joe-ee! Joe-ee! Joe-ee!' He could smell the velvet turf and hear the singing. 'Joe-ee! Joe-ee!' he muttered to himself, making his own crowd noises.

Mr Murphy watched him from a distance, shook his head and sighed. Then cold air froze his knees and icy water turned his toes to ice cubes and the teacher's heart began to sink. Maybe playing Joe was a mistake?

'Play wide on the left wing, Joe,' said Mr Murphy. 'Don't come inside unless I tell you.'

Joe jogged out towards the motorway fence and the game started. One half of the team played against the other. Sken ended up on the opposite side from Joe.

Joe slipped and slid up and down the wing but he never got a pass, nor did Sken. Just give me one shot, thought Joey. Just one. In his mind he could see the ball fly like a bullet from his boot. He imagined how it would flash away and *smack!* hit the back of the net.

After twenty minutes, Joe knew that he would never get a pass, let alone a shot. In the end, he got fed up. I'm going in the middle, he thought. I'll have a better chance of a shot there. So off he went. There was nothing to lose.

His team was attacking down the right. Eddy Morgan ran past a defender and was going to centre. Joe imagined the ball coming towards him. He thought about it flying off his head low into the net. He could already hear the crowd cheering ...

'Joe!' Eddy shouted.

The ball was screaming towards him but it was much too high and fast. If only he had stayed where he was! Too late! Joe tried to jump but his worn boots let him down. The ball hit him on the head like an icy snowball, smashing him down in the sludge before flying out of play.

Eddy came racing over to put his flat nose and skinhead close to Joe's face.

'Why weren't you out there where you were supposed to be?' he snarled. 'You mucked it up!'

Joe just shrugged, 'I ... just ...'

Eddy grunted like a chimp and stomped off. Joe walked away with a headache and a painful lump.

'I think that's enough for today, lads!' shouted Mr Murphy.

The light was now bad. Joe walked off slowly, whistling to cheer himself up.

'Do you have to whistle?' asked Tank.

'No,' said Joe. 'Why? Is it unlucky?'

'It is when you're whistling,' snapped Tank. 'It means that you're on the team.'

'Leave it out!' Arthur, the big keeper, cut in.

'He's as much use as a chocolate teapot,' growled Tank in disgust. Eddy and Tank walked away muttering.

'I can do this,' Joe said to himself. 'I can! If only I had proper boots. If only the others passed to me. If only it wasn't so dark!'

Skenner came up to Joe as he went into the changing room and peered at him in the darkness.

'I shouldn't have missed it!' groaned Joe.

'Don't worry, Joe,' he said. 'You looked all right to me.'

Joe wasn't fooled. It was a bad miss.

CHAPTER 2

Practice makes perfect

That night Joe did not hang around to chat. As he left, he had one last look at the muddy field lit by the hall lights. Then he walked away from the school. Soon it vanished behind the green mist.

Inside, the *boom-boom-boom* of feet told Joe that the gymnastics hadn't finished. However, he wasn't interested. He only had eyes for the football pitch.

Soon he was passing Ashton's Sports, its windows lined with gleaming football boots. Joe whistled when he saw the prices. There was no chance of buying any.

His mum and dad were saving for a holiday. Christmas wasn't far off either. There was no money to chuck around. No money, no boots.

Still, he could dream, couldn't he? Feel their softness round his toes? Smell their new leather? Tank owned three pairs. Joe heard him talking about them.

Finally, Joe jogged away through the chill and soon he was home.

'Everything all right?' said his mum.

'Oh, yes, Mum. I'm playing football for the school next week.'

'For the school?' coughed his dad, almost dropping his paper. 'I'm so pleased, Joe!'

I've got to do well, thought Joe.
Got to.

That night he went slowly upstairs to his room. There, posters of his idols smiled down on him – all strikers.

He stared at them and, as he did, his mind started floating away. He was dancing past people, doing overhead kicks and leaving defenders for dead.

'Yehhh!' he yelled, punching the air as he scored another daydream winner – and knocked the lampshade down.

Crump! The door opened.

'Drink, Joe?' smiled his mum, standing in the doorway with a steaming mug of tea in a Manchester United cup.

His face was hotter than the brew. He booted the fallen shade under the bed. Would she notice the bare light? Mum said nothing.

What a dreamer he was! When Mum had gone he looked in the mirror. He looked at his black hair sprouting like a lavatory brush, his long arms and legs and his huge kipper feet.

'Come on, Joe!' he said to himself, 'do it!'

He had a week in which to practise, a week in which to sort himself out.

Next day, Tank and Eddie started joking about the missed header.

'What wears water-skis, has two shoulders but no head? Joey Jones!'

'What's the difference between Joey Jones and a calendar? A calendar knows what day it is!' and so on.

'How many did you score, Tank?' was all Joe said. Tank scowled.

At the end of the day, he went home. He told his mum he wanted a late tea, got changed and went off to Peel Park alone with his football.

'Having a game with the lads?' asked his dad as he went out.

'No, Dad. It's just me tonight. The others can't make it,' he lied.

When he got there, the place was empty and sad. There was just him and the hulking lines of trees, looming like ghosts in the gloom.

At first, he stomped around, booting the ball up and down, scuffing up the yellow leaves. *Thud! Thud!* He could run all right and give the ball a good crack but it felt like messing around. If only I knew what I was doing wrong, he thought. I'm sure I could do better.

He found a place where there were two trees just about as wide as a goal. Behind them was a high wall. Here he could practise without having to run too far for the ball after each shot.

Great! Now he cracked the ball as hard as he could. Right, left, right, left. When he hit the mark he could hear that Wembley crowd chanting, 'Joe! Joe! Joe!' The trouble was he missed the target ten times as often as he hit it. Then he could hear those same crowds booing and chanting, 'You're-a-load-of-rubbish!'

What was wrong? The slippery boots didn't help.

After another half-hour, the mist was drifting like snow across the park, the trees were black towers, and Joe was worn out.

Suddenly he saw two figures standing in the fog. People were watching.

'Don't stop,' said a familiar voice.

'Yes,' said the taller figure, 'perhaps we can join you?'

'Sken! Mr Skelly?' gasped Joe, amazed. Sken and his dad were standing there. 'What are you doing here?'

Skenner coughed. 'Well, I'm no good but ... I don't like Tank laughing at me. We thought we'd have a kick-about. Fancy a game?'

Suddenly, Joe didn't feel alone any more. Suddenly, energy surged through his body.

'Yes, great! I'd really like to,' replied Joe. 'I want to practise. I want to show Tank too.'

First one lad then the other had a go at beating Mr Skelly who was in goal.

Sken was accurate with his shots but he didn't have power. Big Joe thumped it hard but hit the ball all over the place.

'Hang on!'

Sken's dad brought the practice to a halt.

'Let's see you kick a dead ball,' he said to Joe. 'Take a penalty.'

Joe didn't let on how tired he was and had a go. The ball flashed past the man in a blur – but it missed the goal.

'What a shot!' Mr Skelly said. 'But you look up as you kick the ball. That's why it's going wide.'

'I can hardly stand up in these things!' Joe pointed to his great battered boots.

'Forget the boots! Keep your eye on the ball.'

Whap! Joe took a mighty crack at the ball and it sailed way above Mr Skelly's head.

'That time you kept your eye on the ball but you leaned back,' said Skenner.

'Yes,' Sken's dad called. 'Get your head over the ball.'

The next shot was low and fast. It flew straight past Mr Skelly into the goal.

Joe did it half-a-dozen times. He was still slipping but he was hitting the mark more often.

'Now try heading,' said Mr Skelly.

He lobbed the ball.

Joe raced in and *boom!* hit it hard. It flew quite a way.

'Ow!' yelled Joe because he still had a bump on his forehead from his miss in practice.

His friend's dad came up to him.

'You know something, Joe? You're better than you think. But you've got to believe you can do it.'

'What about me, Dad?' asked Skenner.

'Boggy pitches are a bit heavy for you, son, but I've watched Flowery before. They chase the ball all over the place. When they're worn out, that's when you should get going.'

Sken smiled and Joe thought hard. Mr Skelly knew what he was talking about. Joe didn't mind boggy pitches. And he was a good runner, even if he was clumsy. A plan was forming in his head about the game.

For the rest of the week, Joe practised with Sken and his dad, concentrating on his kicking. Sometimes Joe hit the ball straight. Sometimes it went wide again. But it seemed that the more he believed he could do it, the easier it was.

I'm not a joke now, thought Joe. Not a joke at all! But a practice wasn't like a real match and his boots were still not giving him enough grip.

He should have told his mum and dad about it straight away but, of course, he didn't. He was always shy to ask for things.

Finally, late on the night before the match, he could hold himself back no longer.

'Dad, I haven't got any proper football boots ...' he said.

'Ah,' said Dad. 'I might be able to help you there.'

At the words, Joe's heart leapt. New boots! he thought. He's got me some new boots! He must have got me them for Christmas, thought Joe. But now that I'm in an important match, he's giving them to me early.

Wonderful!

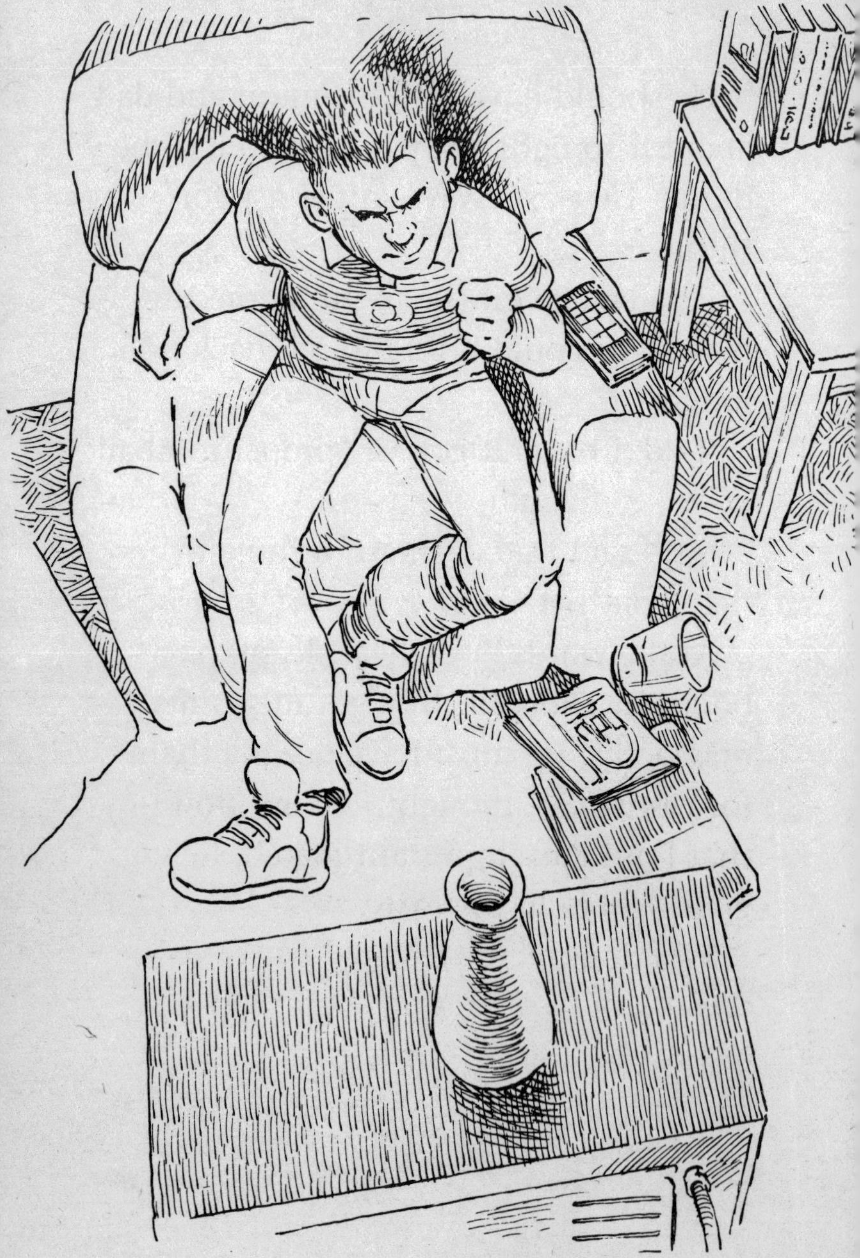

CHAPTER 3

Big boots

Dad went upstairs. Joe excitedly tried to watch the football preview on TV. He wasn't playing for Manchester United or Liverpool, of course, but he was part of it all now; part of the thrill.

His legs twitched with every kick on the screen. His head jerked with every centre. And all the time, his mind was racing ahead to his own great game the next morning, in his super new boots.

It was ages before his dad came downstairs again. He plonked a gigantic pair of shiny black boots in front of Joe.

As he stared at them, the boy felt as if someone had poured ice into his brain.

The boots were awful!

'Good, eh?' said his dad.

Joe found it hard to speak. He had never seen anything like them before.

They weren't low-cut and bendy, soft or supple. They had big, hard square toes, great big long studs and they were high at the ankle. They were his dad's old rugby boots, polished up.

Joe's mind was buzzing with disappointment. They had been good boots, quality boots. And they were his size. Joe's feet were enormous for his age. But he could imagine what everyone at school would say.

'They're ...,' he finally gasped, 'exactly my size.'

At least I won't slip, he thought, the studs are like sharks' teeth! But he couldn't help thinking about the beauties in Ashton's windows. Real boots, not Noddy boots.

That night, he went to bed early but he didn't sleep much.

The wind moaned outside and Barney, his dog, moaned at the end of the bed. Dad coughed next door and Mum snored. He wouldn't have slept much anyway, because he was so terrified of being late.

He woke at 1.17, 2.49, 3.27, 3.43, 4.55. The numbers jumped off the big face of his digital clock. Then 10.40! Ahhh!!!!

He leapt up.

This time he had nodded off. He grabbed the clock. 6.03! 10.40 had been only a dream. At eight, breakfast time, it was raining like mad.

'Might get called off, Joe,' suggested his mum.

'Nay, Mother, it's not like cricket,' said his dad. 'Takes a lot to stop football.'

Joe checked his kit for the tenth time. He put his boots at the very bottom of his holdall, well out of sight. He had decided to put them on when nearly everyone had left the changing room. Then people like Tank wouldn't make fun of him. Soon, it was time to set out.

'See you!' he said.

'Good luck!' said his mum giving him a kiss.

His dad had his coat on, ready for his morning deliveries. 'Want a lift to school?' he said. 'I hope to get down to watch you when I've done the trip to Eccles.'

'Okay,' said Joe.

As Dad's van carried him down the hill to school, Joe was thinking about the boots. If only ... but no, he had to stop that kind of thinking. It doesn't matter about the boots, he told himself.

They'll be covered in mud in no time anyway. They'll grip. They'll kick. Think about the game.

Still, he couldn't help wondering what Tank was going to say.

'Good luck!' said his dad. 'See you later!'

As Joe walked along the school drive he shivered. Suddenly fright ran all over him.

He felt like running away – but then he'd have to come back on Monday to tell the team why he left them one short.

He couldn't back out now. He *had* to know if he had really improved. He walked slowly towards the school.

Once inside, Joe changed into the blue and white of Newton Hall. He felt pure joy when he pulled the shirt over his head. He was playing for the school.

Maybe he'd only ever play once but at least he could say, 'I played for Newton Hall.'

Sken was facing him. He, too, looked happy and surprised.

They both looked up at the same second and burst out laughing.

Sken jogged happily out. Nobody expected anything from him.

Now there was only Joe and Arthur, the man-mountain goalkeeper, left. The big boy always came out last.

He had a yellow T-shirt, knee pads, elbow pads, ankle bandages and a collection of a dozen lucky charms he always kept in the back of the net.

In the end, Joe could not delay any longer. He just had to bring out the monster boots.

Arthur goggled. 'By 'eck, Joe, them's atomic boots!' he grinned.

'My dad's.'

Arthur stood, picked up his lucky charms, his cap and his gloves. Then he gave Joe a little pat on the face with his huge hand.

'Come on, Joe! Let's have some fun, eh?'

And out they clattered into the cold.

CHAPTER 4

Mud pies

Outside, Tank and Eddy just stared at Joe's feet. Then they began braying like donkeys as they scoffed at his boots.

'Look at them,' roared Tank. 'Where did you get them, Jurassic Park?'

'No, Tank,' chuckled Eddy, 'they're not that new!'

Joe felt his ears going red but he said nothing.

When Tank had stopped sniggering, he spoke to Joe and Skenner. 'You two, just keep out of my way, okay?'

Then Mr Murphy told Joe to stay wide on the left. So out Joe stayed. Skenner joined him. It was easier to avoid the clogging mud there.

Tank met Mark Bentley, the other captain, in the middle of the swamp. Mr Murphy tossed for ends, Mark called 'heads'. It wasn't his lucky day.

'We'll play with the tide,' laughed Tank, pointing at the mud.

'Don't get smart with me, Torkington!' snapped Mr Murphy, who wasn't in the mood for jokes. He turned to the other lad. 'Okay. You choose.'

'Hang on, you can't do that, sir! I won the toss!' Tank was purple now.

'And I'm the ref!'

Tank looked up at Mr Murphy's grim face and knew he couldn't win.

Flowery kicked off.

And so began a terrible game of football on a terrible day. The ball soon became a great leaden Christmas pudding that nobody, not even Tank, could kick more than a few metres.

Joe and Skenner never found out if they could or couldn't move it. They hardly even saw the ball. Nobody bothered to pass it to them at all.

To start with, everybody kept their positions. But soon there was almost a scrum round the ball. Only the two keepers plus Skenner and Joe kept clear.

Mud splattered in every direction. In the first ten minutes, there wasn't one shot at either goal.

Arthur started picking his nose in boredom. The other goalie was throwing mud pies at the goalposts to keep warm.

In no time at all, Flowery's canary-coloured shirts were yellowy-black and all Newton's players were blacky-blue – except the two outcasts on the wing, that is.

Finally, just on the stroke of half-time, Joe had a chance.

The ball flew behind the Flowery goal off a defender's slippery boot. Corner! On Joe's side.

At once, Eddy Morgan ran from the other wing to take it.

'It's my kick!' protested Joe.

'Get out of my way. You're not mucking this one up!' Eddy snapped.

Joe backed off. Splat! When Eddy hit the ball, it sounded like a wet cabbage. The ball squirted less than five metres before it stopped.

Eddy fell over backwards and slid along on his bottom. Everyone collapsed with laughter.

A Flowery defender thumped the ball out again.

Corner, again.

Eddy squelched into the middle with his shorts dangling down to his knees, like a wet nappy.

'You take it, Noddy Big Boots!' he sneered.

Joe put the ball on a little pile of mud, like a golf tee. He stepped back. Five paces, ten.

One-two-three-four … Joe ran in hard at the ball and whacked it with his left foot. It went zooming across the middle. The keeper came out but it skidded off his fingers and out of play on the far side.

The others goggled at where the ball had gone.

Mr Murphy blew for half-time. Tank said nothing.

CHAPTER 5

Runaround or hero?

At half-time, as they sucked their oranges, Joe looked hopefully for his dad but he was nowhere to be seen.

Joe and Sken huddled together.

'They're never going to pass to us, you know. I don't want to hang around on the wing any longer,' said Joe.

'Yes …' but before Sken could say anything more, a mud ball splatted into his back.

Tank stood glowering. Mr Murphy was over on the other side of the pitch talking to Flowery's teacher.

'What was that for?' Sken gave Tank a hard look.

'It was to tell you that I'm fed up with you two wandering around like sheep on the wing whilst we do all the work.'

'So?' asked Joe.

'Help the defence!' snapped Tank.

'I'll think about it,' said Joe.

Tank took a step forward. Then he gave Joe a dirty look and stalked off. Joe noticed that Mr Murphy was coming over.

'You two,' said the teacher, 'help the defence. There doesn't seem to be much doing out in the middle.'

Joe groaned inside. He wanted to help the team but he saw no sense in going even further back. Arthur hadn't had one shot to save.

However, he did as he was told. He went back to the edge of the pond in front of Arthur's goal. Sken joined him.

The second half began. And, at first, Joe had nothing to do. The ball was still stuck around the centre circle where Tank and the other boys flopped about like elephants in a water hole. Then, ten minutes from the end, there was danger.

Arthur had booted the ball out but it went nowhere.

The goal was empty. The big Newton keeper was bogged down and the ball bounced just in front of Mark Bentley, the Flowery striker, who wound up a long-range shot.

B-Boom! The great shot sailed up and up over Arthur's head.

Then, it powered down and down and down, to come whizzing at Joe as he ran backwards to defend the open goal.

He had no time to think.

He just flung himself upwards and backwards like a dolphin.

Whumph! The ball smashed into his head like a brick and zoomed away towards the goal.

'Oooooo!' There was a great shout. Joe hardly dared look.

Where was the ball?

Was it behind him in the back of the net? No! The bar was twanging but the net was empty. He glanced down the field. Arthur was booting the ball out to Eddy on the wing.

Arthur waddled back to his goal like a huge bear. He patted Joe on the back.

'Great stop, Big Man! What a header!'

Others shouted, too, but Tank stared silently. Suddenly, Joe felt alive.

He could feel his face burning red and the pain in his head. 'Play back,' 'Leave it alone,' 'Do this, do that!' He was sick of it. Okay, he thought. Now it's my turn! Now, I'll play my game.

He started to go for everything. Suddenly everyone seemed to be moving in slow-motion. But the truth was that the others were very tired.

Joe could run and he hadn't done much to wear himself out.

'Ten minutes, lads! Hang on!' yelled the Flowery teacher. 'And watch that big kid! He's walking all over you!'

Suddenly, Joe was everywhere, a magnet for the ball. Tank stopped sulking and was up there with him.

They set up a chance to score but Tank's shot wasn't strong enough. It beat the keeper but stuck on the line in the mud. Now, it was Tank's turn to have a red face. If only it had been my shot, thought Joe.

By this time, Flowery were as mobile as garden gnomes and Newton Hall weren't much better. Tank and Joe battled on.

But there was still no goal. The match was starting to look like a 0-0 draw.

Then, in the last minute, Newton had a free kick on the edge of the Flowery penalty area.

People started to mark each other. Joe ran up to take the kick but Tank shook his head. 'No chance!' he called. 'This one's mine.'

Joe charged into the middle but Sken shouted to him.

'No, Joe, they've left a gap at the back!'

Joe realized that his friend was right. He took up a position beyond all the defenders and a little way out towards the wing.

Just as the ball was being placed, Joe started to have dreams of glory again. Then he thought, No, No! Stop it, stop this rubbish, Joe! Concentrate!

Tank thundered in for his moment of glory. *Thud!* He had meant to shoot – instead, the ball squirted sideways off his boot right across the face of the goal.

Over came the ball, flying like a great spotty, slimy cannonball straight at Joe.

The rest of the players were stranded, stiff scarecrows in the sludge of the penalty area.

Joe and his great boots stood alone, ten metres out.

'Hit it!' Joe's dad's voice cut the air, as Joe gave the ball a mighty thump with his right boot. Away it zoomed like a greasy pinball, through attackers and defenders alike, into the top corner of the net.

'Yehhhh!' Newton were shouting and racing at Joe, dragging him, slapping him on the back.

'Great goal, Joe!'

'A belter, Joe!'

No insults now! He tried to speak but his mind was all numb.

'You all right?' asked Mr Murphy as Joe counted his bruises.

But Joe didn't reply. Suddenly he was racing like mad towards his own goal.

Newton Hall were so tired that they had hardly gone beyond the half-way line. They thought the game was over.

But there was a great muddy gap between them and Arthur, the big goalie. Mark Bentley had spotted this and when Flowery kicked off, Craig Johnson, another Flowery player, booted the ball past the Newton team for Mark to chase after.

Danger! Mark was stomping. Arthur was lumbering. Sken was slithering. Joe gritted his teeth. It was a close race for the ball.

Mark and Joe got to it at the same time but Joe's big boot swept across Mark's toes. Wham! Out of play went the ball.

Down went the two players.

Then Mr Murphy blew for time and Newton Hall team jumped in the air shouting. Yehhh!!! Made it!!!!!!

Joe and Mark lay like black starfish in the mud.

'Well played!' said Mark.

'You too,' replied Joe.

Then Joe found himself being hauled to his feet. It was Tank! Joe wondered what he was going to say.

The two big boys were face to face but Tank didn't look him in the eye at first. Instead, he looked at the ground, red-faced. Then he looked up at Joe and gave him a little punch on the arm. 'Sorry, Joe!' he said.

Then it was Eddy's turn to say
something to Joe.

'That goal was a cracker! I always
knew you were a good 'un!'

As they all walked into the school, Mr
Murphy came up and added his praise.

Finally, Joe's dad came up too.

'Well, son, you made it,' he said.

'Me, Skenner and your boots,'
laughed Joe.

Other books you might enjoy:

The Young Oxford Book of Football Stories
James Riordan
ISBN 0 19 275060 7

Football—it's the greatest game in the world . . .

The stories in this book will make you laugh, will make you cry, will make you hold your breath—just like the game!

They're all written by keen fans who follow their local teams all over the country. People like Michael Rosen, Robert Swindells, Michael Parkinson, Barry Hines, and lots more.

. . . a must for fans everywhere.

The Worst Team in the World
Alan MacDonald
ISBN 0 19 275072 0

Reject Rovers are about to make history, the worst kind of history. If they lose one more game they'll claim a place in the record books as the official Worst Team of All Time. Can Kevin 'Panic' Taylor transform his team of no-hopers before Saturday?

How to Survive Summer Camp
Jacqueline Wilson
ISBN 0 19 275019 4

Typical! Mum and Uncle Bill have gone off on a swanky honeymoon, while Stella's been dumped at Evergreen Summer Camp. Guess what? She's not happy about it!

Things get worse. Stella loses all her hair (by accident!), has to share a dorm with snobby Karen and Louise, and is forced into terrifying swimming lessons with Uncle Pong! It looks as if she's in for a nightmare summer—how can Stella possibly survive?

Cool Clive, the coolest kid alive
Michaela Morgan
ISBN 0 19 275070 4

Two stories about Cool Clive, the coolest kid alive. In the first story Clive sees a pair of trainers he's just got to have to round off his cool image. But how can he ever earn enough money to buy them? And in the second story find out what happens when Clive goes on a school trip on a hot summer day. Will he be able to keep his cool in all this sun?

Simone's Letters
Helena Pielichaty
ISBN 0 19 275087 9

When ten-year-old Simone starts writing letters to Jem Cakebread, the leading man of a touring theatre company, she begins a friendship that will change her life . . . and the lives of all around her: her mum, her best friend Chloe, her new friend Melanie—and not forgetting Jem himself!

The Bongleweed

Helen Cresswell

ISBN 0 19 275032 1

Warning—Bongleweed on the loose!

The Bongleweed plant is weird and wonderful, and it grows faster than *anything*! Becky tricks stuck-up Jason into sprinkling some seeds in Pew Gardens—but fun soon turns to fear as a bushy Bongleweed jungle springs up, with no sign of stopping.

Before long, the Gardens and local graveyard are completely covered—and now the Bongleweed is heading for the rest of the village! It's up to Becky and Jason to stop the wickedly wild weed before it's too late . . .

A magically funny story from the award-winning author of *The Bagthorpe Saga*.

The Piemakers

Helen Cresswell

ISBN 0 19 275031 3

Arthy, Jem, and Gravella Roller are the finest pie-makers in Danby Dale, famed for their perfect pastry and fantastic fillings. So when they're asked to make a special pie for the king, which will feed two hundred people, the Rollers are thrown into a frenzy of excited preparations. This will be the best ever Danby Dale pie! But unfortunately, wicked Uncle Crispin, a rival pie-maker, has different plans for the Rollers' pie . . . plans that include an extra-large helping of pepper . . .

This funny, charming story was Helen Cresswell's first children's book, and was nominated for the Carnegie Medal.

Temmi and the Flying Bears
Stephen Elboz
ISBN 0 19 275015 1

Temmi is furious when the Witch-Queen's soldiers come to the village to steal one of the flying bears—even more so when he discovers that they've taken Cush, the youngest cub, who is Temmi's favourite bear. Temmi is determined to rescue Cush, but instead finds himself captured and taken to the Ice Castle where he will be a prisoner, too. Escape seems impossible—unless Temmi can somehow win over the ice-hearted Queen . . .

'Stephen Elboz is an exciting new literary talent'

The Independent

Ghostlands
Stephen Elboz
ISBN 0 19 275092 5

From the moment Ewan arrives at Doctor Malthus's house he realizes this will be no ordinary visit. For a start there is Ziggy . . . who's a ghost! And where there is one ghost, there are bound to be others . . .

The local ghost-nappers are out to get Ziggy and are not above a spot of devious magic to help them. And just what has Ghostlands, the nearby theme park, got to do with all this?